Big Sister Now

For my mother, Dorothy Harland Metcalf — A.S.

For Nikki and the staff at N.D., with special thanks to Natalie — K.M.

Published by
MAGINATION PRESS
An Educational Publishing Foundation Book
American Psychological Association
750 First Street, NE
Washington, DC 20002

For more information about our books, including a complete catalog,
please write to us, call 1-800-374-2721, or visit our website at www.maginationpress.com.

Editor: Darcie Conner Johnston
Designer: Michael Hentges
The text type is Candida
Printed by Worzalla, Stevens Point, Wisconsin

Library of Congress Cataloging-in-Publication Data

Sheldon, Annette.
Big sister now : a story about me and our new baby / written by Annette Sheldon ; illustrated by Karen Maizel.
p. cm.
"An Educational Publishing Foundation book."
Summary: "A little girl gets used to sharing her parents with her baby brother and realizes there are some benefits to being a big sister now.
Includes a Note to parents"—Provided by publisher.
ISBN 1-59147-243-1 (hardcover : alk. paper) — ISBN 1-59147-244-X (pbk. : alk. paper)
1. Infants—Juvenile literature. 2. Brothers and sisters—Juvenile literature. 3. Parent and child—Juvenile literature. I. Maizel, Karen, ill. II. Title.

HQ774.S54 2005
306.875'3—dc22

2005005839

10 9 8 7 6 5 4 3 2

Big Sister Now

A Story About Me and Our New Baby

written by **Annette Sheldon**
illustrated by **Karen Maizel**

Magination Press · Washington, D.C.

Always before, when Mommy and Daddy said
"the baby," they meant me. I liked being the baby.
It felt warm and safe and lovey.

Now everything is different.

Now I have a baby brother.

His name is Daniel.

Now when Mommy and Daddy say "the baby," they mean
Daniel. And now when people talk to me, they say,
"Congratulations, Kate, you're a big sister!"
I don't know how to be a big sister. It feels all different.

Everybody is taking care of Daniel all the time. And bringing him presents.

Even my Grandma, the one who calls me her Angel,
calls every day to ask, "How is Daniel?"

I feel like they forgot me.

One morning I needed Mommy to get the bowl for my cereal.

But Mommy was busy feeding Daniel.

11

Mommy said, "Daniel is very hungry. He doesn't know how to wait yet because he is just a baby. You're the big sister now, Kate. Try to be patient for a few more minutes. Then I can help you."

I had to wait.

When Daniel finally finished his breakfast, Mommy got my special bowl and my green pitcher. I poured the milk on my cereal all by myself. I felt very big.

Mommy said, "Kate, I'm proud of you for waiting patiently. Sometimes big sisters have to do that. I know it's hard." I don't like to wait. But I do like to feel big.

One afternoon I needed Mommy to read a book, but Daniel was crying.

So Mommy had to rock him. She rocked and rocked. Daniel cried and cried.

I had to wait. I waited and waited.

While Mommy rocked,
I brought Daniel's new blanket.

18

Daniel still cried.

I brought Daniel's new brown bear.

Daniel snuffled.

I rocked the bear.

Finally, Daniel fell asleep.

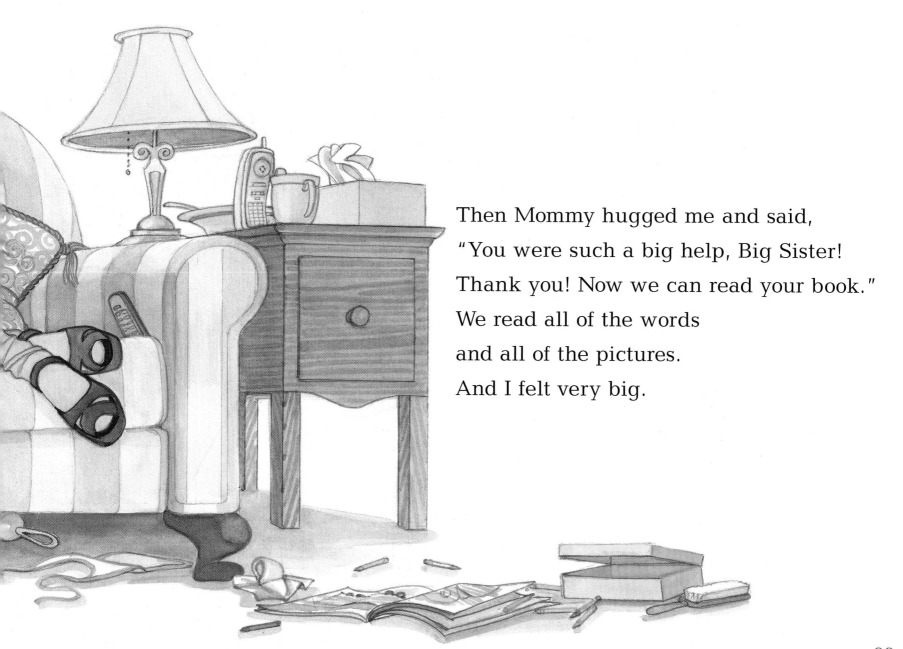

Then Mommy hugged me and said,
"You were such a big help, Big Sister!
Thank you! Now we can read your book."
We read all of the words
and all of the pictures.
And I felt very big.

On Saturday, Daddy and I stayed home with Daniel while Mommy
went to the store. We had lots of fun. My dog Wagner did, too.
We used the broom! And paper towels!

When Daddy changed the diaper I made funny faces and sillies for Daniel.

After Daniel was all fixed up,

Daddy kissed my cheeks and said,

"You are a terrific big sister now!

Look how you made him laugh!"

And then we did our special kitchen dance,

just Daddy and me.

This morning Grandma called to talk to me. "Kate," she said,
"I'm looking for someone who's big enough to help me bake cookies."

Daniel wouldn't be much help. He's still a baby.

But I can do it, so I'm going! I'm the big sister now.

And it feels warm
and safe and lovey.

Note to Parents

by Jane Annunziata, Psy.D.

A new baby in the family is a source of joy for everyone. Older brothers and sisters usually welcome the arrival with their own brand of excitement, wonder, pride, caring, and affection, just as their parents do. At the same time, however, their world is changing in ways they don't understand and can't control, and along with such changes comes an array of less happy feelings, including anger, jealousy, resentment, confusion, and fear that Mom and Dad don't love them as much now.

Older children may express these negative feelings by regressing—by behaving like a baby and wanting to be treated like one. They may also act out their anger by throwing tantrums, pinching the baby, or breaking the baby's toys or their parents' things. Or they may do just the opposite and try to be the perfect child or perfect big sister or brother, trying to regain the spot they fear they've lost in their parents' hearts. These feelings and reactions can be intense—and they are entirely normal, if not inevitable. In addition to keeping a sense of humor, here are a few things that parents can do to help ease the transition.

Before the Baby Arrives

Prepare your older child about the baby before the arrival, and start earlier rather than later. Advance work goes a long way toward helping the older child's adjustment.

Visit the hospital with your child, and take advantage of any sibling classes your hospital or doctor may offer to demystify the event and soothe your child's anxiety.

Let your child know who will be caring for him or her, how long Mom will be gone, when Dad will be home, when the child can visit Mom and see the baby, and any other questions he or she may have.

Concrete, visual reminders are especially comforting. Write out the plan and post it. Even children who are too young to read are reassured by its existence and can ask to have it read and reread to them.

After the Baby Is Home

Set aside one-on-one time with your older child as much as possible. Even if it's just 15 minutes a day or one afternoon a week, exclusive time with Mom and Dad, separately and together, is important. Tell your child how glad you are to have this special time together.

Tell your child stories about him or her as a baby, and look at photographs and other mementos. This will help the child feel as cherished as the new baby.

Gently and at appropriate moments, remind your child of the benefits of being "bigger." You can say, "Babies only get to drink milk. They can't eat ice cream like you do," or "Your sister is too little to go swimming with us. She won't be able to go until she is bigger like you." This can help when the child is feeling jealous or wants to be a baby.

Include your child in some decisions, both before and after the arrival. When children have some say ("Should we buy a yellow blanket or a striped one?"), they feel more involved. This can help with feelings of lack of control. Be careful not to overdo, though. This can lead to resentment about all the special purchases and time being spent on the baby.

Keep the same rules, rituals, and schedules that you had before, so that the world stays as predictable and stable as possible. Expect to have rules challenged more than usual, however.

Try not to change the older child's room, which can cause feelings of displacement. If you must move the child, do it months before the arrival. And if the child is moved or has to share a room with the baby, give him or her as much control as possible with furnishings and so forth. Even a simple line of masking tape or a curtain hanging in the middle of the room can help preserve a sense that "at least part of this is still mine."

Explain what a baby can and cannot do so that fantasies aren't disappointed. An ideal way to do this is to cuddle up together and read books or pamphlets about babies, reminiscing and telling stories about the older child while you read.

Ask your child for help from time to time—bring a diaper or sing a song to the baby. If the child wants to push the stroller or hold the baby, facilitate doing so safely and make sure the rules are clear. This fosters the child's feelings of importance and helps establish sibling bonds.

Avoid giving your child too much responsibility, which can cause resentment. On the other hand, if a child seeks excessive responsibility, trying to win your love, give lots of reassurance that you love him or her just the way he or she is. Tell the child that being the parent is your job, not the child's, even though he or she may be a big sister or brother now.

Offer fun alternatives when the child can't do something because of the baby. For example, if the baby is sleeping and the child must be quiet, offer to bake cookies or read a book together.

Address as much as possible your child's valid complaints about the baby. If the baby wakes the child at night, for example, look for solutions such as shutting the door or running a noise screen. Not only does the problem get solved, but the child also learns that the parents are devoted to meeting his or her needs as well as the baby's.

When the going gets rough, as it often does, it may help to remember that your child is behaving in ways that are to be expected. It can even be calming to the child to be told directly, "It's okay to feel mad at your brother sometimes. All children feel that way when they're getting used to a new brother or sister."

✱

Jane Annunziata, Psy.D., is a clinical psychologist with a private practice for children and families in McLean, Virginia. She is also an author of several books addressing the special needs of children and parents.

About the Author
Annette Sheldon is a storyteller, preschool specialist, and librarian. She lives with her husband and a free-spirited English setter on a small farm in nearby Austinburg, Ohio. The Sheldons have four children and ten grandchildren. This is Annette's first book.

About the Illustrator
Karen Maizel began her career as a fashion illustrator. In raising three daughters, her interest crossed over into their world of children's books and magazines. Although her children are grown, she continues to be passionate about creating pictures for anyone who is young or young-at-heart, and has illustrated 14 books. Karen lives in Lakewood, Ohio, with her family.